ASTERIX IN BELGIUM

TEXT BY. GOSCINNY

DRAWINGS BY UDERZO

TRANSLATED BY ANTHEA BELL AND DEREK HOCKRIDGE
with apologies to:
George Gordon, Lord Byron, Mr Wm. Shakespeare, Mr John Milton
and
Pieter Breughel the Elder

HODDER DARGAUD
LONDON SYDNEY AUCKLAND

ASTERIX IN OTHER COUNTRIES

Australia	Hodder Dargaud, Rydalmere Business Park, 10/16 South Street, Rydalmere, N.S.W. 2116, Australia
Austria	Delta Verlag, Postfach 1215, 7 Stuttgart 1, West Germany
Belgium	Dargaud Bénélux, 3 rue Kindermans, 1050 Brussels, Belgium
Brazil	Record Distribuidora, Rua Argentina 171, 20921 Rio de Janeiro, Brazil
Canada	Dargaud Canada, 307 Benjamin Hudon, St Laurent, Montreal H4N 1J1, Canada
Denmark	Serieforlaget A/S (Gutenberghus Group), Vognmagergade 11, 1148 Copenhagen K, Denmark
Esperanto	Delta Verlag, Postfach 1215, 7 Stuttgart 1, West Germany
Finland	Sanoma Corporation, P.O. Box 107, 00381 Helsinki 38, Finland
France	Dargaud Editeur, 12 Rue Blaise Pascal, 92201 Neuilly sur Seine, France *(titles up to and including Asterix in Belgium)* Les Editions Albert René, 26 Avenue Victor Hugo, 75116 Paris, France *titles from Asterix and the Great Divide, onwards)*
Germany, West	Delta Verlag, Postfach 1215, 7 Stuttgart 1, West Germany
Holland	Dargaud Bénélux, 3 rue Kindermans, 1050 Brussels, Belgium *(Distribution)* Van Ditmar b.v., Oostelijke Handelskade 11, 1019 BL, Amsterdam, Holland
Hong Kong	Hodder Dargaud, c/o United Publishers Book services, Stanhope House, 13th Floor, 734 King's Road, Hong Kong
Hungary	Nip Forum, Vojvode Misica 1-3, 2100 Novi Sad, Yugoslavia
India	*(Hindi)* Gowarsons Publishers Private Ltd, Gulab House, Mayapuri, New Delhi 110 064, India
Indonesia	Penerbit Sinar Harapan, J1. Dewi Sartika 136D, Jakarta Cawang, Indonesia
Israel	Dahlia Pelled Publishers, 5 Hamekoubalim St, Herzeliah 46447, Israel
Italy	Dargaud Italia, Via M. Buonarroti 38, 20145 Milan, Italy
Latin America	Grijalbo-Dargaud S.A., Deu y Mata 98-102, Barcelona 29, Spain
New Zealand	Hodder Dargaud, P.O. Box 3858, Auckland 1, New Zealand
Norway	A/S Hjemmet (Gutenburghus Group), Kristian den 4des gt 13, Oslo 1, Norway
Portugal	Meriberica, Avenida Alvares Cabral 84-1° Dto, 1296 Lisbon, Portugal
Roman Empire	*(Latin)* Delta Verlag, Postfach 1215, 7 Stuttgart 1, West Germany
Southern Africa	Hodder Dargaud, P.O. Box 548, Bergvlei, Sandton 2012, South Africa
Spain	Grijalbo-Dargaud S.A., Deu y Mata 98-102, Barcelona 29, Spain
Sweden	Hemmets Journal Forlag (Gutenberghus Group), Fack, 200 22 Malmö, Sweden
Switzerland	Interpress Dargaud S.A., En Budron B, 1052 Le Mont/Lausanne, Switzerland
Turkey	Kervan Kitabcilik, Basin Sanayii ve Ticaret AS, Tercuman Tesisleri, Topkapi-Istanbul, Turkey
USA	Dargaud Publishing International Ltd, 2 Lafayette Court, Greenwich, Conn. 06830, U.S.A.
Wales	*(Welsh)* Gwasg Y Dref Wen, 28 Church Road, Whitchurch, Cardiff, Wales
Yugoslavia	Nip Forum, Vojvode Misica 1-3, 2100 Novi Sad, Yugoslavia

Asterix in Belgium

ISBN 0 340 25735 0 (cased)
ISBN 0 340 27753 X (limp)

Copyright © Dargaud Editeur 1979, Goscinny-Uderzo
English language text copyright © Hodder and Stoughton Ltd 1980

First published in Great Britain 1980 (cased)
This impression   91 92 93

First published in Great Britain 1983 (limp)
This impression   91 92 93

Published by Hodder Dargaud Ltd,
Mill Road, Dunton Green, Sevenoaks, Kent TN13 2YA

Printed in Belgium by Proost International Book Production

GAULISH VILLAGE

COMPENDIUM

LAUDANUM

AQUARIUM

TOTORUM

ARMORICA

BELGICA

LUTETIA

S.P.Q.R.

GAUL
(ROMAN CONQUEST)
50 B.C.

CELTICA

AQUITANIA

PROVINCIA

The year is 50 BC. Gaul is entirely occupied by the Romans. Well, not entirely... One small village of indomitable Gauls still holds out against the invaders. And life is not easy for the Roman legionaries who garrison the fortified camps of Totorum, Aquarium, Laudanum and Compendium...

a few of the Gauls

Asterix, the hero of these adventures. A shrewd, cunning little warrior; all perilous missions are immediately entrusted to him. Asterix gets his superhuman strength from the magic potion brewed by the druid Getafix...

Obelix, Asterix's inseparable friend. A menhir delivery-man by trade; addicted to wild boar. Obelix is always ready to drop everything and go off on a new adventure with Asterix — so long as there's wild boar to eat, and plenty of fighting.

Getafix, the venerable village druid. Gathers mistletoe and brews magic potions. His speciality is the potion which gives the drinker superhuman strength. But Getafix also has other recipes up his sleeve...

Cacofonix, the bard. Opinion is divided as to his musical gifts. Cacofonix thinks he's a genius. Everyone else thinks he's unspeakable. But so long as he doesn't speak, let alone sing, everybody likes him...

Finally, Vitalstatistix, the chief of the tribe. Majestic, brave and hot-tempered, the old warrior is respected by his men and feared by his enemies. Vitalstatistix himself has only one fear; he is afraid the sky may fall on his head tomorrow. But as he always says, 'Tomorrow never comes.'

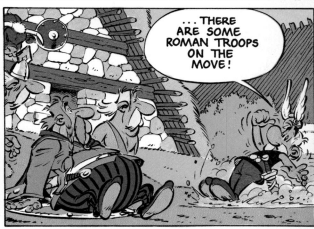

5

YOU KNOW, IT'S A FUNNY THING ABOUT THE ROMANS: WE'RE SO PLEASED TO SEE THEM, AND THEY'RE ALWAYS SO ANNOYED WHEN THEY HAVE TO COME HERE...

SSH! THEY'RE COMING! LET'S HIDE!

WHEN GAIUS COMES MARCHING HOME AGAIN, HURRAH, HURRAH... MENHIR A NEW DAY WILL COME MY WAY...

THEY LOOK PLEASED, ASTERIX!

YOU DON'T, OBELIX.

IT'S PLANE INFURIATING... I SHALL NEVER BE IN CONCORDE WITH THE ROMANS!

LET'S GO AND TELL OUR CHIEF.

SOON AFTER-WARDS...

PLEASED? ARE YOU SURE?

YES, O CHIEF. THEY WERE SINGING. VERY BADLY, BUT THEY WERE SINGING.

HM... IF THE ROMANS ARE FEELING HAPPY, THAT'S BAD NEWS FOR US. MAYBE THEY'VE INVENTED A SECRET WEAPON.

WHO CARES? WE'VE GOT OUR OWN SECRET WEAPON: YOUR MAGIC POTION, O DRUID!

YES, AND YOU'RE GOING TO TAKE SOME, BECAUSE YOU'D BETTER GO AND SEE WHAT'S UP IN THE FORTI-FIED ROMAN CAMPS.

I KNOW, I KNOW: I FELL INTO THE SECRET WEAPON WHEN I WAS A BABY, ETC., ETC.

LET'S GO AFTER HIM AND QUESTION HIM.

HEY, YOU!

?

OH, SOME GAULS.

LEAVE THIS TO ME.

?

WELL, ARE YOU GOING TO ANSWER? *ARE YOU GOING TO ANSWER?*

SLAP SLAP SLAP SLAP

STOP IT, OBELIX. LET GO OF HIM.

HOW DO YOU EXPECT HIM TO ANSWER BEFORE WE'VE ASKED HIM ANYTHING?

YOU HAVE A POINT THERE!

HOW LOVELY TO BE BACK HERE AGAIN... WHAT WAS IT YOU WANTED TO KNOW, BY THE WAY?

LOVELY?

I WANT TO KNOW WHY YOU'RE SO HAPPY. WHAT'S THE IDEA?

WE'RE JUST BACK FROM CAMPAIGNING AGAINST THE BELGIANS...

AND WE'RE SO GLAD TO HAVE LEFT THEIR COUNTRY! THAT'S WHY WE'RE HAPPY. JULIUS CAESAR SAID THE BELGIANS ARE THE BRAVEST OF ALL THE GAULISH PEOPLES, AND HE WAS ONLY TOO RIGHT...

?!

SO WE'RE BACK HERE FOR A REST CURE.

A REST CURE?

THEY'RE SENDING ROMANS HERE FOR A REST CURE?

AND THE LEGIONARY TOLD US THAT AFTER THE BELGIANS, EVEN OBELIX THUMPING HIM WAS LOVELY.

AND THEY KEEP TELLING FUNNY STORIES ABOUT BELGIANS. THERE WAS ONE ABOUT KNOCKING NAILS INTO WALLS WITH THEIR HANDS, THE WAY I ALWAYS DO!

THERE'S NO NEED TO GET UPSET; I THINK IT'S RATHER PLEASING TO KNOW THE ROMANS COME HERE FOR A REST CURE.

RATHER PLEASING?

IF THIS SORT OF THING GOES ON, WE'LL HAVE EVERYONE COMING TO THE ARMORICAN COAST FOR THEIR HOLIDAYS TO ENJOY THE BRACING AIR, THE COUNTRYSIDE, THE FOOD...

WE'RE TURNING INTO A HOLIDAY CAMP FOR ROMANS, AND HE THINKS IT'S RATHER PLEASING! MAKES YOU WONDER IF IT WAS WORTH FIGHTING THE BATTLE OF GERGOVIA AT ALL!

DON'T GET SO UPSET, PIGGYWIGGY. IT WAS ONLY A COMMON LEGIONARY'S OPINION. JULIUS CAESAR VALUES YOU AT YOUR TRUE WORTH.

THE FACT IS...

THE FACT IS WHAT?

JULIUS CAESAR SAID THE BELGIANS WERE THE BRAVEST OF ALL THE GAULISH PEOPLES.

OH, SO THAT'S WHAT CAESAR SAID, IS IT? RIGHT, YOU KNOW WHAT I THINK OF CAESAR?

PIGGYWIGGY, IF YOU WANT TO BE COARSE, GO AND BE COARSE ELSEWHERE!

YOU BET I WILL! I'M CALLING A VILLAGE COUNCIL MEETING STRAIGHT AWAY!

I'VE SUMMONED YOU BECAUSE I'M FED TO THE TEETH WITH HEARING ABOUT THESE BELGIANS CAESAR THINKS ARE SO BRAVE...

OH, I THOUGHT YOU'D SUMMONED US TO FEED US TO THE TEETH WITH WILD BOAR...

LOOK, WE'RE ONLY JUST STARTING THIS STORY. IT'S MUCH TOO SOON FOR THE BANQUET, AND ANYWAY, THE BARD IS STILL WITH US.

SHUT UP, YOU TWO CLOWNS! I SUGGEST WE GO AND SEE THESE BELGIANS AND FIND OUT WHAT'S SO SPECIAL ABOUT THEM!

BONK!

AND THEN WE'LL SHOW THEM WE'RE THE BRAVEST. AND CAESAR, TOO! WHAT DO YOU THINK OF THAT?

NOT A LOT.

IF THE BELGIANS ARE BRAVE, GOOD FOR THEM AND TOO BAD FOR CAESAR. WE'D DO BETTER TO MIND OUR OWN BUSINESS!

GETAFIX IS RIGHT! ARTISTIC VALUES MATTER MORE THAN BRUTE FORCE. I MEAN, LOOK AT ME...

MY WIFE DOESN'T LIKE ME TO GO AWAY ON MY OWN... SHE HAS SUCH A JEALOUS NATURE!

PERSONALLY, I AGREE WITH THE DRUID.

RIGHT, SO THAT'S THE END OF THE STORY, AND WE CAN TIE UP THE BARD AND BRING ON THE BOAR!

WELL, IF THAT'S HOW YOU FEEL, I'M OFF TO SEE THE BELGIANS ON MY OWN!

I'LL SHOW EVERYONE THAT THE BRAVEST OF ALL THE GAULISH PEOPLES IS ME!

I THINK YOU AND OBELIX HAD BETTER GO WITH HIM, OR THIS STORY MAY COME TO A STICKY AS WELL AS A PREMATURE END.

*Amiens

SO WHAT'S THE BIG JOKE, AND WHO ARE YOU JOKERS, ANYWAY?

I'M A VETERAN OF GERGOVIA. WE'RE FROM ARMORICA, AND...

ARMORICANS.

THOUGHT SO, FROM THEIR ARMORICANISMS.

AND YOU'RE BELGIANS?

THAT'S RIGHT. YOU'RE LIKELY TO MEET BELGIANS IN BELGIUM.

WE'RE DIVIDED INTO BELLOVACI, SUESSIONES, EBURONES, ATUATUCI, NERVII, CEUTRONES, GRUDII, LEVACI, PLEUMOXII, GELDUMNES, AND MENAPII, BUT WE'RE ALL BELGIANS.

I HEAR YOU'RE AT WAR?

AFTER WEEKS BENEATH THE CONQUEROR'S YOKE, WE DECIDED WE WEREN'T STANDING FOR IT ANY MORE!

WELL, WE'LL BE ON OUR WAY. THERE'S A ROMAN CAMP TO BE RASED TO THE GROUND BEFORE DINNER.

CAN WE COME WITH YOU?

YOU WANT TO COME AND WATCH? WHAT FOR? YOU NEED LESSONS?

LESSONS?

WE DON'T NEED ANY LESSONS FROM ANYONE!!!

ALL RIGHT, BUT YOU MUSTN'T GET IN OUR WAY. YOU AND YOUR MEN STAY AT THE BACK WHERE IT ISN'T DANGEROUS.

WELL, DID YOU ENJOY IT?

ACTUALLY, THAT WAS JUST TO ANNOY THEM A BIT. WE LET THE GARRISON GO FREE, SO THEY CAN TELL THEIR FRIENDS, AND IT WON'T DO THEIR MORALE A BIT OF GOOD!

HM, YES, NOT BAD AT ALL.

NOT BAD!

SAY THAT AGAIN! YOU THINK YOU LOT COULD DO ANY BETTER??

NO NEED TO FLY OFF THE HANDLE...

I MEAN YOU HANDLED THAT LITTLE ATTACK QUITE WELL! OF COURSE WE COULD DO BETTER.

OH YES? RIGHT, IF YOU THINK YOU CAN DO BETTER, I'D JUST LIKE TO SEE YOU TRY!!!

GOT ANOTHER LITTLE ROMAN CAMP AROUND HERE?

YES, PLENTY. WE'LL GIVE YOU ONE, WON'T WE, MATES?

TEEHEEHEE!

COMING?

YOU'RE VERY HOSPITABLE!

CHEERS, O CHIEF VITAL-STATISTIX!

HM? OH, YES!

GLUG GLUG GLUG GLUG

CRAAASH!

IT IS A TRICK! IT IS A TRICK!

SLAP! SLAP! SLAP! SLAP!

I FEEL QUITE AT HOME HERE. THEIR LEGIONARIES ARE JUST LIKE OURS.

SOON AFTER-WARDS...

WELL... I THINK THAT'S OVER.

ALREADY? BUT WE'VE ONLY JUST BEGUN!

HAVE THEY GONE?

SSH! KEEP STILL.

COME ON, BOYS! I CAN'T WAIT TO SEE THE BELGIANS' FACES.

WELL, HOW DID YOU LIKE THAT, BELGIANS?

NOT BAD. QUITE AMUSING.

WHAT DO YOU MEAN, QUITE AMUSING?

NOW, SERIOUSLY, WHY DID YOU COME TO VISIT US?

OH, IT WAS ONLY BECAUSE OF SOME SILLY REMARK JULIUS CAESAR MADE. HE'LL HAVE HAD HIS TONGUE IN HIS CHEEK TOO.

SCRUNCH!

WELL, WHAT WAS IT? DON'T HOLD YOUR TONGUE NOW!

APPARENTLY HE SAID THE BELGIANS WERE THE BRAVEST OF ALL THE GAULISH PEOPLES.

RIDICULOUS!

WHAT DO YOU MEAN, RIDICULOUS?

SCRUNCH!

BECAUSE WE'RE QUITE AS BRAVE AS YOU, IF NOT MORE SO!

SCRUNCH!

18A

JULIUS CAESAR NEVER TELLS LIES! WE'RE THE BRAVEST!

OH, SO THAT'S THE LIE OF THE LAND, IS IT? JULIUS CAESAR IS A LIAR! WE'RE THE BRAVEST!

I'M NOT TAKING A LIE LIKE THAT LYING DOWN!

COME ALONG, BE REASONABLE! WE'RE ALL THE BRAVEST, AND THAT'S THAT.

IF YOU'RE THE BRAVEST, YOU'LL HAVE TO PROVE IT!

JUST WHAT I WAS ABOUT TO SUGGEST! LET'S HAVE A COMPETITION!

A COMPETITION? AND WHO'LL JUDGE THE COMPETITION?

JULIUS CAESAR, OF COURSE!

18B

SIT DOWN, EVERYONE. SUPPER'S READY!

THAT NIGHT...

I DON'T LIKE THE IDEA OF THIS COMPETITION TOO MUCH. IT COULD BE A STICKY BUSINESS AFTER ALL.

I LIKE THIS COUNTRY, AND I LIKE THE PEOPLE TOO. THEY STICK AT NOTHING! LET'S GO TO SLEEP. I DON'T WANT TO BE LATE FOR BREAKFAST-AND-LUNCH.

GOOD NIGHT, ASTERIX!

GOOD NIGHT, IDIOTIX!

NEXT MORNING...

COME AND GET IT!

HERE'S THE MAP SHOWING THE ROMAN CAMPS ROUND ABOUT. NOW, I SUGGEST YOU ATTACK THE CAMPS TO THE NORTH AND WE ATTACK THE CAMPS TO THE SOUTH.

SCRUNCH, SCRUNCH, SCRONCH!

AND WE'LL SEE WHO KNOCKS DOWN THE MOST!

IF CAESAR'S GOING TO REFEREE THE MATCH, WE MUST MAKE SURE WE IDENTIFY OURSELVES TO THE ROMANS.

AND TO BE PERFECTLY HONEST, I OUGHT TO TELL YOU WE USE A MAGIC POTION. IF YOU'D CARE FOR A DROP...

NO, WE DON'T NEED ANY OF THAT! OUR BEER IS STRONG ENOUGH FOR US!

I'LL MAKE SOME SANDWICHES. YOU CAN'T GO OFF FIGHTING WITHOUT A PACKED LUNCH, DINNER AND SUPPER.

LATER, IN A ROMAN CAMP TO THE NORTH OF THE BELGIAN VILLAGE...

THERE ARE THREE MEN AND A DOG APPROACHING THE CAMP!

SIX MEN GO OUT ON PATROL AND SEE WHAT THEY WANT!

23

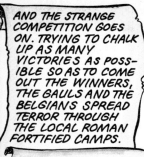

AH, WE'RE JUST THIS MINUTE BACK! WE'VE DESTROYED ALL THE CAMPS ON OUR SIDE OF THE VILLAGE!

YOU TOO?

IT'S A DRAW.

WE'LL HAVE TO HAVE A REPLAY.

YOU KNOW, I DO THINK IT MAY HAVE OCCURRED TO SOMEONE TO TELL CAESAR ABOUT TODAY'S EVENTS. WE CAN JUST ASK HIM TO ADJUDICATE BETWEEN US.

THAT'S RIGHT. THE NEXT MEAL'S READY!

BY THE WAY, DARLING, DID YOU EVER THINK OF CUTTING ROOTS INTO CHIPS AND FRYING THEM?

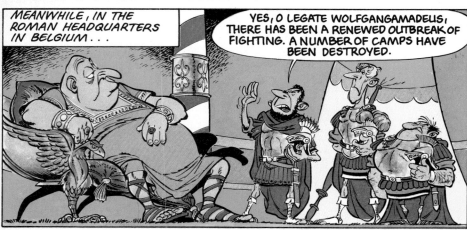

MEANWHILE, IN THE ROMAN HEADQUARTERS IN BELGIUM...

YES, O LEGATE WOLFGANGAMADEUS, THERE HAS BEEN A RENEWED OUTBREAK OF FIGHTING. A NUMBER OF CAMPS HAVE BEEN DESTROYED.

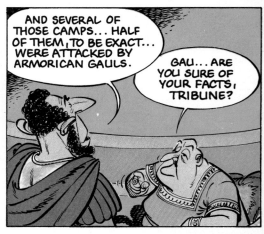

AND SEVERAL OF THOSE CAMPS... HALF OF THEM, TO BE EXACT... WERE ATTACKED BY ARMORICAN GAULS.

GAU... ARE YOU SURE OF YOUR FACTS, TRIBUNE?

YES, O LEGATE. THEY EVEN PUT THEIR SIGNATURE TO THE DAMAGE THEY INFLICT BEFORE SIGNING OFF.

AND ARE THERE MANY OF THESE GAULS?

ALL THE CENTURIONS IN COMMAND OF THE CAMPS INVOLVED AGREE THAT THERE WERE VAST HORDES OF GAULS, ACCOMPANIED BY PACKS OF SAVAGE HOUNDS, AND THEY WERE AIDED BY A MYSTERIOUS FLEET OF NEUTRALS!

THIS IS VERY SERIOUS INDEED! I SHALL START FOR ROME STRAIGHT AWAY TO TELL JULIUS CAESAR!

WE'VE BEEN HERE AT A LOOSE END FOR DAYS! THERE'S NO NEWS OF CAESAR, BEEFIX AND BRAWNIX AND THEIR FRIENDS KEEP NEEDLING US, AND THEY SAY NO ONE EVEN NOTICED OUR BRILLIANT ACHIEVEMENTS!

SUPPOSE WE GO HOME? IT'S NEARLY THE MUSH-ROOM AND TRUFFLE SEASON.

TRUFFLES ARE TRIFLES COMPARED TO OUR MILITARY REPUTATION!!!

HULLO, STILL CROSS, ARMORICAN, OLD FRIEND?

I'M IN NO JOKING MOOD!

WELL, IT'S NOT OUR FAULT IF CAESAR HAS MORE IMPORTANT THINGS TO DO THAN BOTHER ABOUT YOU LOT, IS IT?

IT SHOWS HE KNOWS NOTHING ABOUT MILITARY STANDARDS!

A MAN WHO SAYS WE'RE THE BRAVEST IS A REAL EXPERT WHEN IT COMES TO JUDGING MILITARY STANDARDS, YOU HEAR ME?

RIGHT, WHY DON'T WE FIGHT EACH OTHER INSTEAD OF THUMPING IGNORANT ROMANS WHO DON'T EVEN KNOW A BRAVE MAN WHEN THEY SEE ONE? THEN WE'LL FIND OUT WHO'S THE BRAVEST!

NOT A BAD IDEA, AS YOUR IDEAS GO!

CALM DOWN.

?

?

?

?

Julius Caesar has arrived in Belgium.

To be precise Culius Jaesar has arrived in Gelbium.

31

* BRASSICA OLERACEA BOTRYTIS

WAKE UP, LEGIONARY. WE COME WITH A FLAG OF TRUCE, AND WE'D LIKE TO SEE CAESAR. SORRY WE KNOCKED BEFORE ENTERING.

A LITTLE LATER...

YES...IT'S A FLAG OF TRUCE ALL RIGHT.

?!

?!

I TOLD YOU THEY WERE SAVAGES HERE!

ALL RIGHT, SEND THEM IN, AND LET'S KEEP CALM.

THAT'S YOUR FLAG OF TRUCE, IS IT? FUNNY... I HAVE A FEELING I'VE SEEN YOU SOMEWHERE BEFORE, BUT NOT IN BELGIUM.

WELL, YOU SEE, WE AREN'T BELGIANS; WE COME FROM ARMORICA.

SO IT WAS TRUE! ALL THE GAULS ARE REVOLTING!

ALL THE GAULS? NO, JUST OUR ONE SMALL VILLAGE, STILL HOLDING OUT AGAINST THE INVADERS...

BUT YOUR CHIEFS SURRENDERED! IT'S TREASON! YOU'RE LIVING AT OUR EXPENSE OFF THE FAT OF THE LAND!

NO, WE'VE BEEN LIVING OFF THE BELGIANS. THEY'RE THE FAT OF THE LAND. I'M JUST WELL COVERED MYSELF.

WELL, IF YOU'VE COME TO SURRENDER, I MAY YET PROVE MERCIFUL...

NO, NO. IT'S JUST THAT WE HAD A COMPETITION, AND WE'D LIKE YOU TO BE THE ADJUDICATOR.

PFFFF!

COMPETITION?: ADJUDICATOR!?

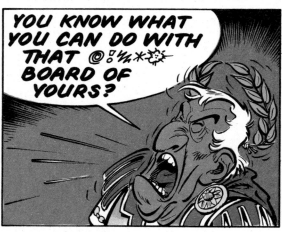

PREPARATIONS FOR THE GREAT BATTLE BEGIN...

LEGATE WOLFGANGAMADEUS, ONCE BATTLE HAS BEEN JOINED YOU AND YOUR COHORTS ATTACK THE ENEMY IN THE REAR!

I HEAR AND OBEY, O CAESAR. I'LL BE OFF.

UMBELLIFERUS, I AM PUTTING YOU IN CHARGE OF MY IMPERIAL GUARD. THEY WILL TAKE PART ONLY IN THE LAST RESORT. WE SHALL OPEN FIRE WITH OUR CATAPULTS!

MAY THE GODS LOOK DOWN UPON US WITH FAVOUR!

ALEA JACTA EST!

AND AS FOR YOU, I'LL SEE YOU IN MY OFFICE AFTER THE BATTLE!

THE BELGIANS ARE GETTING READY FOR BATTLE TOO. FAST RUNNERS ARE SENT TO ROUSE THE NEIGHBOURING TRIBES...

BONANZA, DID YOU TRY THAT IDEA OF MINE ABOUT FRIED CHIPPED ROOTS?

NO, THE MENAPII INSISTED ON COOKING THE LAST MEAL BEFORE THE BATTLE. THEY WANTED A NICE WATERZOOI TO SOUP THEM UP.

WATERZOOI! WATERY STUFF FOR MEN WHO WANT CAESAR TO MEET HIS WATERLOO!

WITH JULIUS CAESAR AT THEIR HEAD, MARSHALLED IN PERFECT ORDER, THE LEGIONS, MAINTAINING STRICT MILITARY STANDARDS, MARCH OFF TO THE BATTLEFIELD.

THE BELGIANS, WITH BEEFIX AND BRAWNIX AT THEIR HEAD, ARE MAKING FOR THE FATEFUL BATTLEGROUND TOO...

WHAT SORT OF PROVISIONS ARE THERE IN THE BAGGAGE TRAIN?

BEER AND SANDWICHES.

WHAT'S THE FILLING IN THE SANDWICHES?

WHOLE COLD ROAST OXEN.

BUT HARK!

OUR TROOPS ARE IN POSITION.

OUR CATAPULTS ARE LINED UP.

36A

THAT HEAVY SOUND BREAKS IN ONCE MORE...

FIRE!

BING!

BONG!

BING!

BONG!

ARM! ARM! IT IS—IT IS—THE CATAPULT'S OPENING ROAR!

WHAT SORT OF BING-BONG BALLS WERE THOSE?

36B

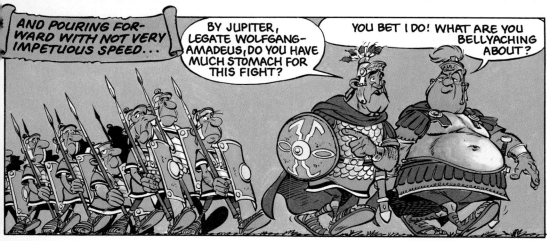

AND POURING FORWARD WITH NOT VERY IMPETUOUS SPEED...

BY JUPITER, LEGATE WOLFGANG-AMADEUS, DO YOU HAVE MUCH STOMACH FOR THIS FIGHT?

YOU BET I DO! WHAT ARE YOU BELLYACHING ABOUT?

I DON'T TRUST THESE BELGIANS, AND OUR MEN AREN'T TOO HAPPY EITHER. I'M AFRAID WE MAY BE LURED INTO A TRAP.

SO THEY'VE CHUCKED US OUT! OH, OF COURSE WE'RE ONLY FOREIGNERS, AREN'T WE? WE DON'T HAVE ANY RIGHT TO OUR BIT OF FUN! TALK ABOUT XENOPHOBIA!

DO CALM DOWN...

EVER SINCE THE START I'VE BEEN TELLING YOU THIS IS NONE OF OUR BUSINESS. SURELY YOU KNOW HOW THEY FEEL?

ALL I KNOW IS THAT I WANT TO BASH SOMEONE OVER THE HEAD! IT'S ALL VERY WELL BEING TACTFUL, BUT IF I CAN'T BASH SOMEONE OVER...

SSH!

I THINK YOU MAY BE ABLE TO LET OFF STEAM AFTER ALL; THERE ARE ROMANS COMING!

THERE, SEE THAT? YOU CAN RELY ON THE ROMANS! THE ROMANS TAKE LIFE SERIOUSLY.

LOTS OF ROMANS TOO! WE'D BETTER FINISH UP OUR MAGIC POTION.

GLUG! GLUG!

GLUG! GLUG! GLUG!

WE'LL MEET THEM IN THAT LITTLE WOOD OVER THERE...

IT'S A TRAP ALL RIGHT! A VAST HORDE OF BELGIANS!

NO, NO, WE'RE GAULS FROM ARMORICA.

AND A PACK OF HOUNDS!

BIFF! BAFFF! DOIINNNG! BONNK! GRRR WOOF! WOOF!

COME BACK! WE OUTNUMBER THEM!

COME BACK, BY JUPITER! THEY'RE ABOUT TO OUTNUMBER ME!

I KNOW YOU! YOU'RE ARMORICANS! YOU HEARD WHAT CAESAR SAID: YOU'VE NO RIGHT TO TAKE PART IN THIS BATTLE!

SPEAKING OF BATTLES, HOW COME YOU'RE NOT TAKING PART?

DZZING!

CAE... CAESAR WANTED ME TO TAKE THE BELGIANS IN THE REAR, BUT I WON'T IF YOU DON'T WANT ME TO...

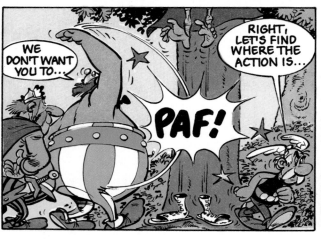

WE DON'T WANT YOU TO...

RIGHT, LET'S FIND WHERE THE ACTION IS...

PAF!

OH, BUT WE HAVEN'T BEEN INVITED...

COME ON. THEY'LL BE NEEDING REINFORCEMENTS BY NOW.

BUT YESTERDAY THE WORD OF CAESAR MIGHT HAVE STOOD AGAINST THE WORLD... HOWEVER, THAT DAY HE DID NOT OVERCOME THE NERVII, OR THE MENAPII, OR ANYBODY ELSE. CAESAR IS NO LONGER IN A POSITION TO JUDGE ANYTHING...

IN FACT, CHAOS UMPIRE SITS, AS THE OCCUPYING FORCES SOON REALISE:

FAREWELL, CAESAR! OUR OCCUPATION'S GONE!!!

DO YOU SURRENDER?

NO! UP GUARDS AND AT 'EM!

OH NO, WE DON'T!

THESE ROMANS ARE CRAZY!

BUT UP GUARDS AND...

YOU KNOW WHAT THE GUARD WILL BE PUBLISHING TO THE WORLD ABOUT YOU?

PUBLISH AND BE DAMNED.

RIGHT. I'M BACK OFF TO ROME. I'M RELYING ON YOU TO KEEP THIS LITTLE AFFAIR AS QUIET AS POSSIBLE...

A HORSE FOR CAESAR.

AND IT IS A CASE OF RUIN UPON RUIN, ROUT ON ROUT, CONFUSION WORSE CONFOUNDED....

RUN FOR YOUR LIVES! RUN! RUN FOR IT!

WE'RE THE GREATEST RUN-MAKERS! WE WON THE MATCH! THEY'LL NEED MORE THAN RUNNING REPAIRS AFTER THIS!

THE WAY'S BARRED.

IF YOU INTEND TO KILL ME, BARBARIANS, I WARN YOU THAT I SHALL SELL MY DISTINGUISHED LIFE DEARLY!

NO, THAT'S NOT THE IDEA AT ALL...

IT'S ABOUT OUR COMPETITION...

YOU'VE SEEN US IN ACTION, SO NOW WILL YOU ADJUDICATE? WHO ARE THE BRAVEST?

I'VE NO IDEA WHO ARE THE BRAVEST! ALL I KNOW IS THAT YOU'RE ALL EQUALLY CRAZY!!!

AND NOW I'M GOING BACK TO ROME, AND I DON'T WANT TO BE BOTHERED ANY MORE! OFF WE GO!

PFFFFFF

PFFFFFF

HAHAHA! HOHOHO!

COME ON BACK TO THE VILLAGE, AND WE'LL HAVE A LITTLE PARTY TO CELEBRATE!

WHAT ON EARTH IS THAT?

NO IDEA...A SOUVENIR I PICKED UP ON THE BATTLEFIELD!

LOOKS LIKE A SEASIDE SOUVENIR...IT EVEN HAS MUSSELS STILL STICKING TO IT.

MUSSELS...THAT'S FISHY ...FISH...WONDER HOW FISH WOULD GO WITH CHIPPED ROOT VEGETABLES?

AND THERE IS A SOUND OF REVELRY BY NIGHT.

IT IS TIME FOR OUR FRIENDS TO LEAVE...

COME TO MY ARMS, ARMORICANS!

...AND RETURN HOME TO THE WELCOME DUE TO HEROES...

DID YOU REMEMBER MY MACKEREL?

WELL, YOU BROUGHT OUR FIRE-EATING CHIEF BACK IN GOOD HEALTH, BUT WHAT WAS THE RESULT OF THE COMPETITION?

YOU MIGHT SAY IT WAS A TIE BETWEEN US AND THE BELGIANS!

AND THE STORY ENDS HAPPILY FOR OBELIX AND ALL HIS FRIENDS, SINCE, WHEN THERE IS PLENTY OF BOAR ON THE GROANING BOARD, NONE OF THE GAULS ARE EVER BORED.

HOW WAS THE BELGIANS' LITTLE PARTY?

VERY PICTURESQUE. JOY WAS UNCONFINED.

TU-WOO?

GOSCINNY & UDERZO.

48

proost Turnhout (Belgium)

PRINTED IN BELGIUM